Look Back!

Trish Cooke

Illustrated by Caroline Binch

First published in 2013 by Papillote Press
23 Rozel Road, London SW4 0EY
www. papillotepress.co.uk
www.facebook.com/papillotepress

Paplllote Press would like to acknowledge the help of Sonia Riviere and the late Lorna Jno Baptiste

Design by Andy Dark

Printed in China

A catalogue record for this book is available from the British Library

ISBN 978-0-957-1187-2-0

Papillote Press
London and Roseau, Dominica

For my Mum who made me laugh with her stories
For my Dad who made the Bolom real for me...
Trish Cooke

For Eeva and Adam in Dominica
For Malala 'the bravest girl'
Caroline Binch

'I ever tell you about Ti Bolom?' Grannie asked.
Christopher shook his head.

'Eh Kwik!' Grannie called.
'Eh Kwak!' Christopher answered.

Christopher always answered that way because
Grannie had told him that was the way stories
had been told to her in Dominica.

'Well,' Grannie said, 'I have heard that Ti Bolom is
short, short, short, his foot long, long, long and flat,
flat, flat. He has a big head and two big black eyes
and when you walking alone at night, minding your
own business, Ti Bolom walks behind you,

pattaps pattaps...
huh huh huh.

But when you turn around...he's not there. He's gone!

'Eh Kwik!' Grannie called.
'Eh Kwak!' Christopher called back.

'Well,' said Grannie, 'One time, when I was
about your age, I had to bring some food
for an old lady who lived down the way from us.
Her name was Ma Constance.

'It was still light outside but I knew it would be dark
on my way back. I had heard stories about the
mischievous Ti Bolom who walked about at night
and I was 'fraid. But I didn't let Mammy know
because I wanted to show her that I was a big girl.

'When I reach by Ma Constance,
I say, "Bonsoir, Ma Constance, is
me Christophine. My Mammy
send me with some food for you."
I give Ma Constance the food
and I go quick, quick, quick.

'Eh Kwik!'
'Eh Kwak!' said Christopher.

Outside it was getting dark.
The moon was out and the
crickets were singing.

'I walk, I walk and every step I take
I hear footsteps behind me...
a big long foot slapping the ground...

pattaps pattaps...

and the sound of short breaths...

huh huh huh.

I was real 'fraid, I break into a run.
I run, I run and

bladdaps! I fall down.

'And that's when I see it…'

'What!' cried Christopher. 'What did you see? Was it Ti Bolom?' Christopher asked full of fear.

'There was some long grass and the grass was moving, like something was hiding there…

'But when I look in the long grass,' Grannie said, 'there was nothing there. But I know it was Ti Bolom!'

'But how do you know it wasn't an animal or something?' Christopher asked.

'Animals leave signs, footprints, droppings, tell-tale signs. But not Ti Bolom, he too clever for that! You see Ti Bolom make you know he there, then he make you *think* you dream him but I know what I know! Yes, and I catch him out!

'Eh Kwik!'
'Eh Kwak!

'You caught Ti Bolom?' Christopher asked in amazement.

'Well...' Grannie pondered, 'I set a trap for him.

'The next week, when Mammy send me to take the food for Ma Constance, I dig a hole,' said Grannie,

'….a deep hole and I cover it with grass.

'And that night, on my way home from visiting Ma Constance, when I was sure Ti Bolom was following me, I pretend like I walking over it. But instead of putting my foot in the trap, I take a big step. I miss the trap but I know well Ti Bolom behind me and...

'*Bladdaps!*

Ti Bolom fall down

Bladdaps!

in the hole!'

'*Bladdaps!*'

laughed Christopher.
'You caught Ti Bolom!
You caught him!'

'Well…not exactly,' said Grannie. 'You see
Ti Bolom is smart! While Ti Bolom was in
the hole, he dig and he dig deep until he
make a passage…and he get away!'

'Oh no!' said Christopher.

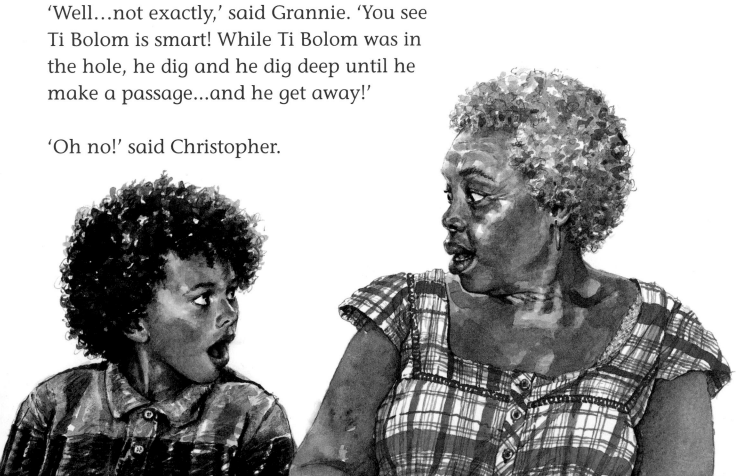

'Oh yes, but I didn't give up. No *sah*. I make a plan. The next time I had to bring food for Ma Constance, I wait for her to finish eating, then I wash out the pot. I scrub it clean and rub a cloth on it 'til the pot shine, shine, shine! Then I carry the pot and I head off back home.

'Eh Kwik!'
'Eh Kwak!' said Christopher.

'It was a full moon and the light was falling right on Mammy's shiny pot making it like a mirror. And when I hold it in a certain way, I could see what was behind me without turning around. So as I walk, I turn the pot this way and that way so I could see Ti Bolom behind me.

'Then…

WOOF

'From out of nowhere a dog bark.
I drop the pot and I run home fast!
After that I was too 'fraid to ever
look for Ti Bolom again!'

'But Ti Bolom!' Christopher
pleaded. 'What happened to him?'

'Ti Bolom? Oh, that little fella is still around, out and about, trying to make fools out of us!' Grannie said chuckling.

'Eh Kwik!'
'Eh Kwak!'

Christopher said nervously.

Around and about where, he wondered, looking over his shoulder for any signs of Ti Bolom.

As Grannie dozed off for her afternoon nap, Christopher thought about what she had told him.

Could Ti Bolom be real or was Ti Bolom just a story Grannie had made up? He was sure *he* had heard the

pattaps pattaps

of Ti Bolom's long flat feet slapping the floor once or twice. And the

huh huh huh

too, following him to the bathroom in the dead of night. But was it really Ti Bolom?

There was only one thing to do – Christopher had to know if Ti Bolom was real. He had to see him face to face.

That night, Christopher hid a torch and a small mirror under his bed. After Mum had turned off the light, he felt for them in the darkness and crept to the bedroom door.

Christopher listened to the sound of his footsteps as they creaked on the floorboards and his heart thumped. Then he heard something else...

pattaps pattaps...

But when he turned around there was nothing.

'Ti Bolom...?' Christopher whispered, 'Is that you?' and then he heard another sound...

huh huh huh.

Christopher clasped his mirror tightly and held it so he could see what was behind him. And there in the beam of the torchlight, reflecting onto the mirror was...

...Ti Bolom!

'Hello!' Ti Bolom said. 'I have
travelled so far to meet you…'
And he grinned.

Then as quickly as Ti Bolom had appeared,
he disappeared again into the place where
only dreamers and story makers know
where to find him…

'Eh Kwik!'
'Eh Kwak!'

Trish Cooke is an award-winning author, scriptwriter and actress of Dominican heritage. Born in Bradford, she was inspired to write mostly by her parents who were great storytellers. Her most popular children's book, *So Much* (illustrated by Helen Oxenbury) won the 0-5 category of the Smarties Book Prize and the Kurt Maschler Award in 1994. She has written plays for stage, TV and radio, and also runs creative writing workshops. See more at www.trishcooke.co.uk

Caroline Binch is an award-winning children's illustrator and author who is probably best known for her illustrations for *Amazing Grace*, which has become an international best-seller. Her book *Hue Boy* (written by Rita Phillips Mitchell) won the Smarties Gold Award in 1993 and *Gregory Cool*, which she wrote and illustrated, was highly commended for the Kate Greenaway medal. Caroline was born in Manchester but now lives by the sea in Cornwall. See more at www.carolinebinch.co.uk

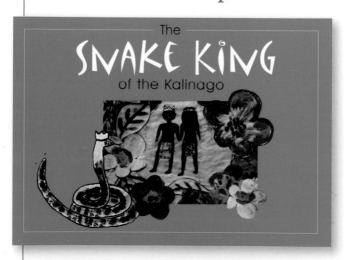